A
LONG
AWAITED
WINTER

JERRY B. MARCHANT

Summary

In a remote village in rural France, James "J.D." Delaney lives a quiet life to atone for past sins. A former spy, he abandoned this world after a mistake cost his brother his life. But his past resurfaces when Irina Volkova, a woman with a mysterious past, demands the classified list of Russian spies he holds. This list, stolen years ago, could cause a global crisis. To survive, J.D. must ally himself with the only person who knows about his dark past. "***A Long-Awaited Winter***" is a story of guilt, courage and redemption. From the frozen French countryside to the dark alleys of Paris, J.D. faces a chess game in which trust is tested and allies can become traitors.In this cold winter, the ghosts of the past finally make themselves heard.

Contents

CHAPTER 1
SHADOWS OF THE PAST

The sun hung low in the sky, casting a golden hue over the snow-covered vineyards of rural France. James "J.D." Delaney stood at the window of his rustic stone cottage, the chill of winter creeping through the glass panes. The landscape outside was picturesque, a postcard of serenity that belied the storm brewing within him. He had built this life of seclusion ten years ago, a deliberate choice to escape the ghosts of his past, yet the shadows of those memories still lingered like spectres in the corners of his mind.

J.D. turned away from the window, his gaze falling on the shelves lining the walls of his modest living room. Each bottle of vintage French wine, meticulously collected over the years, stood as a testament to his resolve against indulgence. He had long since made peace with the fact that he could no longer trust himself with vices. The last time he had allowed himself to indulge—years ago in a dimly lit bar in Kiev—had ended in chaos and bloodshed. He shivered at the thought.

As he moved to the small kitchen, the scent of fresh bread filled the air. He had taken to baking as a form of therapy, a way to ground himself in the present. The loaves were golden brown, a stark contrast to the cold outside. He pulled one from the oven, its warmth wrapping around him like a comforting embrace.

But as he sliced into the crusty exterior, his thoughts drifted back to that fateful mission in Ukraine. The faces of those he had lost haunted him: colleagues, innocents, and the one person who had mattered most —his brother. J.D. had been the analyst, the linguist who had misinterpreted a critical piece of intelligence, leading to a botched operation that cost lives. The guilt had driven him to this isolated life, away from the world of espionage that had once thrilled him.

He placed the bread on the table and poured himself a cup of dark coffee, his hands shaking slightly. The tranquility of his surroundings was abruptly shattered by the distant sound of a car approaching. He frowned, peering through the frosted window. A sleek black vehicle glided to a stop at the end of his driveway.

J.D. felt a knot tighten in his stomach. Visitors were rare in this part of the world, and he had gone to great lengths to ensure his privacy. He set down his coffee, moving cautiously to the door, the Luger P08 already in his hand—a relic from his Berlin days, meticulously oiled. Through the frosted glass, he could see a figure stepping out of the car —tall, poised, and unmistakably confident. The figure moved with purpose, a stark contrast to the rustic charm of his cottage.

The knock came at 5:47 a.m.

Three knocks. Pause. Two knocks. A KGB cadence, outdated but deliberate. Delaney's pulse didn't quicken. He'd rehearsed this moment for years.

Through the rain-streaked window, he sees her: a silhouette sharp as a scalpel, trench coat cinched tight. Ice-blonde hair glints beneath the porch light. *Russian*, he thinks, *but not Moscow—something colder*. Siberia, maybe. Grozny.

He hesitates. Not out of fear, but ritual. Ten years ago, he'd have barricaded the door, fled through the root cellar. Now, he straightens his sweater—gray wool, frayed at the cuffs—and breathes in the scent of bergamot and impending storm. *Showtime.*

(through the door, in French)
—"We're closed. Try the bakery in town. Their lies are fresher."
—"I prefer stale truths, Mr. Delaney. Open the door."

He does. Rain gusts into the cottage, carrying the smell of wet earth and diesel exhaust. Her eyes—pale blue, like Arctic ice—flick to the Luger in his hand. She doesn't reach for her own weapon.

—"I've been waiting for you. What took so long?"

Standing before him was a woman, sharp and striking. Irina Volkova. He recognized her immediately, despite the years that had passed since their paths had last crossed. The scar across her jawline told stories of battles fought and survived, and her piercing blue eyes held a fierce intensity that sent a chill down his spine.

"Delaney," she said, her voice smooth yet edged with steel. "We need to talk."

J.D. took a step back, instinctively placing a hand on the doorframe for support. "What do you want, Irina? I'm not involved in any of this anymore."

"Not involved? You're the only one who can help me," she replied, her tone unyielding. "I know you have it."

He studied her for a moment, the memories flooding back—shared missions, whispered conversations, and the tension that had crackled between them. But that was a lifetime ago.

"I don't know what you're talking about," he said, trying to maintain his composure.

Irina's expression shifted, her eyes narrowing slightly. "You can't lie to me, J.D. I know you speak perfect Russian, and I know you've been living under an alias. The list you stole—it's not just a rumor. The Kremlin wants it back."
His heart raced, and he felt his pulse quicken. The classified list of deep-cover Russian spies was a ghost he had hoped to bury forever. It was a

relic of his past life, one that had nearly cost him everything.

"You don't understand the danger you're in," he said, his voice barely above a whisper. "You need to leave."

Irina stepped forward, her presence commanding. "And let you hide away in this cottage while the world burns? You owe it to those who died because of your mistakes to help me."

J.D. hesitated, the weight of her words sinking in. The ghosts of the past were rising, and he could no longer ignore them. But as he looked into her fierce eyes, he also saw a flicker of something else—an understanding, a shared pain.

"Come inside," he finally said, opening the door wider. "We have a lot to discuss."

As she stepped over the threshold, J.D. felt the chill of winter seep into his bones—a harbinger of the storm that was about to unfold. The past had returned, and with it, the dangerous game of espionage he had tried so hard to escape.

CHAPTER 2
WHISPERS IN THE WIND

The door clicked shut behind Irina, sealing the cold air outside. J.D. felt the weight of her presence in his small living room, the shadows of the past looming large. He gestured toward a worn chair at the kitchen table, while he took a seat opposite her, studying her carefully.

"Coffee?" he offered, his voice steadier than he felt.

"No, thank you," she replied, her gaze unwavering. "Let's get to the point."

He nodded, swallowing hard. "You said something about a list. What exactly do you know?"
Irina leaned forward, her posture tense, as if she were poised to spring into action. "I know that you were the last person to have access to it before it disappeared. The Kremlin is on high alert, and they believe you have it hidden somewhere. They'll do anything to get it back, including sending people to find you."

J.D. felt a knot tighten in his stomach. He had never intended to keep the list; it had been a matter of survival. In the chaos of that fateful night in Ukraine, he had taken it as a precaution, fearing it would fall into the wrong hands. "I don't have it," he lied, the words tasting bitter on his tongue.

Irina's expression hardened. "You're lying, and we both know it. You may think you've escaped, but the past doesn't let go easily. Not for you, not for me."

He leaned back, crossing his arms defensively. "Why should I help you? You're working for the Kremlin, aren't you? This is all just a ruse to get what you want."

She sighed, exasperated. "You don't understand. I'm not here for them. I'm here for my brother. You were responsible for his death, Delaney. That botched operation in Ukraine—it was your mistake that got him killed."

The accusation hung in the air, heavy and suffocating. J.D. felt the blood drain from his face. He could still see the chaos of that night—the gunfire, the screams, the moment he realized it was too late. "I didn't know he was there," he stammered.

"Does that matter? You made a choice, and people died because of it," she shot back, her voice rising with emotion. "But I'm not here to kill you. Not yet. I need you alive to verify the authenticity of the list. If it's legitimate, it could turn the tide in this conflict."

J.D. felt a glimmer of hope mixed with dread. "And if I refuse? What then?"

Irina's gaze softened momentarily. "Then you'll be hunted, just like I am. The Kremlin will stop at nothing to silence you, and I can't protect you if you refuse to cooperate."

He weighed her words, feeling the gravity of the situation. "What's your plan?"

"I have contacts who can help us. We need to verify the list and expose the corruption within both the CIA and the Kremlin. They've turned this into a game of power, and innocent lives are at stake," she explained, her voice steady now, filled with conviction. J.D. felt a flicker of admiration for her resolve. Despite their tumultuous history, Irina had grown into a formidable force. "And what's in it for you?" he asked, genuinely curious.

"Revenge," she said simply, her eyes narrowing. "But also justice. I owe it to my brother to see this through."

Silence enveloped the room as the weight of their shared history settled upon them. J.D. felt the walls closing in, the past and present colliding in a chaotic dance. He had long wanted to atone for his mistakes, but the path ahead was fraught with danger. "Fine," he finally said, breaking the silence. "I'll help you. But first, we need to lay low. If the Kremlin is on our tail, we can't draw attention to ourselves."

Irina nodded, her expression shifting to one of determination. "Agreed. We need to get to the list before they do. Do you have it hidden somewhere?"

J.D. hesitated, knowing that revealing its location meant inviting Irina deeper into his world—a world he had tried so hard to leave behind. "It's hidden, but you need to understand that this is dangerous territory. Once we get involved, there's no turning back."

"I'm aware of the risks," Irina replied, her tone resolute. "I didn't come all this way to back down now."

He studied her for a moment, searching for any hint of hesitation. But there was none. They were both trapped in a web of their own making, and this might be their only chance to find redemption.
"Alright," he said, standing up. "We'll need to move quickly. If we're going to do this, we can't waste any time."
Irina stood as well, a spark of determination igniting in her eyes. "Lead the way."
As J.D. led her to the cramped cellar beneath his cottage, he felt the chill of the past creeping back, wrapping around him like a shroud. The darkness of the cellar was palpable, full of old memories and regrets, but it was also filled with the hope of a new beginning. Together, they would

face the storm that awaited them,
even if it meant confronting their
deepest fears.

And as they descended into the
shadows, J.D. couldn't shake the
feeling that this was only the
beginning of a long, treacherous
winter.

CHAPTER 3
THE CELLAR

The cellar was a small, dimly lit space beneath J.D.'s cottage, accessed through a low, creaky door that seemed to groan with age. The air was cool and musty, tinged with the scent of damp earth and old wood. A single bulb flickered ominously from the ceiling, casting a light that struggled to chase away the shadows clinging to the corners.

As they descended the narrow, winding stairs, J.D. felt the familiar chill wrap around him, a stark contrast to the warmth of the cottage above. The stone walls were rough and uneven, their surfaces dotted with patches of mold. Shelves lined one side of the cellar, filled with dusty jars and forgotten relics from a bygone era. Old tools hung haphazardly on hooks, evidence of a life that had once been vibrant and full of activity.

At the far end of the cellar, a heavy wooden crate caught his eye. It was unmarked and weathered, its edges splintered and worn. J.D. approached it cautiously, his heart pounding as memories flooded back—memories of the choices he had made and the secrets he had kept.

He knelt beside the crate, brushing away layers of dust. With a steady hand, he pried open the lid. Inside lay a steel lockbox wrapped in an RFID-blocking pouch, its nickel fabric neutralizing any remote tracking signals. J.D. ran a calloused thumb over the tamper-evident seal —a strip of adhesive embedded with microscopic glass beads that scattered like diamond dust if disturbed. The beads still glinted intact.

"You hid it here?" Irina muttered, eyeing the mold-streaked walls. "No Faraday cage? No biometric lock?"

"The best security is irrelevance," J.D. said, peeling back the pouch to reveal a keypad. "Four tries before it fries the contents."

0402—his brother's birthday. The lock hissed open.

Irina leaned in as J.D. lifted the folder labeled *Project Dusk*. Beneath the top sheet—a roster of codenames and embassy postings—lay a second layer: pages of seemingly random numbers.

"Steganographic cipher," J.D. said, thumbing a UV penlight clipped to his keyring. Blue beams illuminated annotations in the margins: *'89 Margaux, '03 Pomerol.* "Key's hidden in my wine catalogs. Coordinates correlate to auction lot numbers."

Irina's eyes narrowed. "You expect me to believe the Kremlin's crown jewel is decoded via vintage Bordeaux?"

"The SVR's counter-intel division doesn't stockpile *Wine Spectator*," J.D. snapped, frustration creeping into his voice. "It's deniable."

Suddenly, a muffled thud echoed from above—a floorboard groaning under misplaced weight. Both froze.

"Company," Irina whispered, drawing a micro pistol from her boot, the metal glinting in the dim light.

J.D. snapped the lockbox shut, feeling the weight of their predicament settle in. "Back stairwell. Now."

As they ascended, he palmed a NATO-style lanyard grenade from the crate—insurance for the unexpected. Shadows bled across the walls, winter's teeth biting deeper as they moved swiftly, adrenaline coursing through them. Each creak of the floorboards echoed their urgency, a reminder that time was running out.

Once they reached the top, J.D. paused, listening intently. The muffled sound from above had subsided, but he could still feel the tension lingering in the air.

"Did you hear that?" J.D. asked, exchanging a glance with Irina.

"Yeah," she replied, her voice low. "We need to be ready for anything."

They stepped into the cool air outside, the winter sun hanging low, casting long shadows across the snow-covered landscape. The beauty of the scene was almost surreal, the tranquility of the moment starkly contrasting with the turmoil brewing beneath the surface.

J.D. led the way down a narrow path that wound through the vineyards, his heart racing as he glanced around, half-expecting to see dark figures lurking in the distance. He had always prided himself on being cautious, but now every sound felt amplified, every rustle of branches a potential threat.

"The last thing I want is to draw attention to ourselves," he said, keeping his voice low. "We need to move quickly and quietly."

Irina fell into step beside him, her presence both comforting and unsettling. "I can handle myself, you know. I've dealt with worse than a few prying eyes."

He shot her a sidelong glance. "I have no doubt, but this isn't just about you. We're in deep now, and I can't afford to lose you."

Her lips curled into a slight smirk. "You think I'm a liability?"
"Not a liability. A wild card," he replied, a hint of a smile breaking through his tension. "And I don't know if I can trust you completely. Not yet."

Irina's expression shifted, the playful banter replaced by a seriousness that mirrored his own. "You don't have to trust me, J.D. You just have to believe that we both want the same thing: to survive."

They pressed on through the vineyards, the crunch of snow underfoot their only sound. As they approached the edge of the property, J.D. felt a sense of urgency in the air, a premonition that their time was running out. He glanced over his shoulder, scanning the horizon for any sign of danger.

"Once we reach the road, we should be able to flag down a car," he said, focusing on the task at hand. "We need to act inconspicuously."

Irina nodded, her demeanor shifting back to the calculated operative he had known. "I'll handle the negotiations. Just follow my lead."

They reached the road, a narrow, winding path that led to the nearest town. J.D. glanced at Irina, feeling a mix of admiration and apprehension. "You really believe we can pull this off?"

"Believe? No. But I know we have to try," she replied, her voice firm. "The stakes are too high, and the clock is ticking."

As they stood by the roadside, a vehicle approached in the distance. J.D.'s heart raced as he raised a hand, signaling for the driver to stop. The car slowed, the driver eyeing them with curiosity.
"Just remember," Irina said softly, "no matter what happens, we stick together."

The car that approached was a sleek, silver sedan, its polished exterior glinting in the winter sun. The driver was a middle-aged man, perhaps in his late forties, with salt-and-pepper hair neatly combed back. His angular face bore the lines of experience, hinting at a life lived on the edge. He wore a dark wool coat that contrasted sharply with the crisp white of his shirt, and a patterned scarf wrapped loosely around his neck added a touch of color. His piercing green eyes, sharp and observant, scanned J.D. and Irina with a mix of curiosity and caution.

As he rolled down the window, the faint scent of leather mixed with the freshness of the winter air wafted out. "Can I help you?" he asked, his voice smooth but laced with skepticism.

J.D. noted the way the man's gaze flicked to the side, assessing the surroundings as if he sensed the weight of their situation. There was an air of confidence about him, a quiet authority that suggested he was no stranger to navigating uncertain waters.

"We need a ride to Paris," J.D. said, stepping closer to the window, trying to convey urgency without raising alarm.

The driver raised an eyebrow, clearly weighing his options. "That's quite a journey. What's in Paris that's got you out here in the countryside?"

Irina leaned in slightly, her demeanor shifting to one of charm and persuasion. "Just a little business that requires discretion. We're willing to pay for your trouble."

The man studied them for a moment longer, his expression unreadable.

There was a glimmer of intrigue in his eyes, but also a hint of caution. "Alright," he said finally, a slight smirk forming. "But you'll need to get in quickly. I don't want to hang around here longer than necessary."

As they climbed into the backseat, J.D. felt a mix of relief and unease. The driver put the car in gear, and they sped away from the vineyards, leaving the cottage—and the ghosts of their pasts—behind.

CHAPTER 4
ENCOUNTERS

The car glided smoothly along the winding roads, the rhythmic hum of the engine providing a strange comfort. J.D. sat in the back seat, glancing at Irina, who was already engaged in a quiet conversation with the driver. The man, whose name they had learned was Henri, had proven to be surprisingly amiable, though his eyes still held a cautious gleam.

"Do you have contacts in Paris?" J.D. asked, turning his attention to Irina as they navigated the outskirts of the village.

She nodded, her expression focused. "A few. They're discreet and reliable, but I can't guarantee their loyalty. We'll have to tread carefully."
"What's their connection to the list?" he inquired, needing to understand the stakes of their gamble.

"They work in intelligence, but they're not directly affiliated with the Kremlin or CIA," Irina explained. "They can help us verify the list's authenticity and determine the best way to leak it without attracting too much attention."

J.D. leaned back, processing her words. The plan was risky, but it was their only shot. "And if they decide to turn us in?"

Irina's gaze hardened. "Then we'll deal with it. But I trust them more than I trust most people in this game."

As they approached the outskirts of Paris, the landscape shifted from the quiet countryside to the bustling energy of the city. The streets were lined with cafés and boutiques, the sidewalks filled with people going about their day, oblivious to the storm brewing just beneath the surface.

Henri maneuvered the car through the narrow streets, his demeanor calm and collected. "Where to?" he asked, glancing at Irina in the rearview mirror.

"Drop us off near Avenue de l'Opéra," she instructed, her voice steady. "There's a small café close to the corner—La Belle Époque. We should be safe there."

As they neared the café, J.D. felt a knot of anxiety tighten in his stomach. The city felt different now, charged with a sense of urgency and danger. He had spent years avoiding places like this, where shadows lurked around every corner and allies were often enemies in disguise.

Henri pulled to the curb, and they quickly exited the car. "Thanks for the ride," J.D. said, sliding a few bills into Henri's hand. "We appreciate it."

"Just stay safe," Henri replied, eyeing both of them before driving off. The moment the car disappeared around the corner, J.D. felt the weight of the world settle back onto his shoulders.

They stepped into the café, the warm air enveloping them like a comforting embrace. The scent of freshly baked pastries and robust coffee filled the space, but the atmosphere buzzed with an undercurrent of tension. J.D. scanned the room, searching for any signs of danger.

"Relax," Irina said, lowering her voice as they found a small table in the corner. "We're just here for coffee, remember?"

He nodded but couldn't shake the feeling that they were being watched. As they settled into their seats, a waiter approached, his demeanor polite but indifferent.

"Bonjour, madame, messieur. What can I get for you?" he asked, his French fluid and welcoming.

Irina ordered a coffee and a croissant, while J.D. opted for a black coffee. As the waiter moved away,

J.D. leaned in closer to Irina. "What's the next step?"

"Wait for my contact, Marie. She should be here soon," Irina replied, her eyes scanning the café. "She's trustworthy and knows the ins and outs of the intelligence community in Paris."

"Do you trust her?" he asked, feeling the weight of every decision pressing down on him.

"More than most," she said, her gaze steady. "But remember, trust is a luxury we can't afford right now." They settled into a tense silence, the noise of the café fading into the background as J.D. wrestled with his thoughts. He couldn't shake the feeling that they were on borrowed time, and the rumble of the city outside felt like a countdown.

Just then, the door swung open, and a woman stepped inside, her presence commanding. She was in her thirties, with dark hair pulled back into a sleek bun and sharp features that revealed both confidence and intelligence. She wore a tailored coat and had an air of sophistication about her.

Irina's eyes lit up, and she stood as the woman approached. "Marie," she greeted, a genuine smile breaking through her usual stoicism.

"Irina," Marie replied, leaning in for a quick embrace before shifting her gaze to J.D. "And you must be Delaney. I've heard quite a bit about you."

"None of it good, I hope," J.D. said, forcing a smile as he extended his hand.

Marie shook it firmly, her grip strong. "The past is the past. Right now, we have more pressing matters." She slid into the seat across from them, her expression shifting to one of seriousness. "I assume you have what we discussed?"

Irina nodded, her demeanor shifting back to business. "We need to verify the list's authenticity and formulate a plan to leak it without attracting unwanted attention."

Marie leaned in, her voice low. "Very well. But we need to be cautious. If the Kremlin is after you, they won't hesitate to make a move. We can't afford any slip-ups."

As Irina pulled the locked box from her bag, J.D. felt a surge of anxiety. The stakes had never been higher, and he was acutely aware of the dangers lurking in the shadows. The café buzzed around them, but their little corner felt like a world unto itself—three players caught in a dangerous game, each with their own motivations.

Marie examined the box carefully, her expression unreadable. "This is crucial, but we need to think several steps ahead. The moment this goes public, you'll both be targets."

J.D. felt the weight of her words settle heavily on his chest. "We're prepared for that," he said, trying to inject some confidence into his voice.

"Prepared? Or just hopeful?" Marie countered, her gaze piercing through him. "We can't afford naivety. You need to understand the implications of what you have."

Irina interjected, her tone firm. "We understand, Marie. But we're not backing down. Not now."

Marie nodded, respect flickering in her eyes. "Then let's get to work. We have a lot to discuss, and time is not on our side."

As they delved into the details of their plan, J.D. felt the weight of the world shift. They were no longer mere fugitives; they were players in a dangerous game, and the outcome would determine not just their fates, but the lives of countless others.

Outside, the winter sun dipped lower in the sky, casting long shadows that crept into the café, a reminder that the long, treacherous winter had only just begun.

CHAPTER 5
A GAME OF DECEIT

The atmosphere in La Belle Époque crackled with tension as Marie laid out the plan. J.D. listened intently, aware that every word could tip the balance between success and catastrophe. Irina remained focused, her gaze locked on Marie as they discussed their next moves.

"First, we need to confirm the list's authenticity," Marie said, her tone clipped and professional. "I have a contact within the French intelligence service who can help. We need to get the list to him discreetly, preferably before the end of the day."

"Who is this contact?" J.D. asked, feeling a sense of unease. Trust was a fragile commodity in their world, and he needed to understand the risks involved.

"His name is Philippe," Marie replied. "He's reliable but cautious. He'll want to verify the list before we take any further action. If he vouches for it, we can proceed to leak it to the media."

Irina leaned forward, her expression serious. "And if he doesn't?"

"Then we'll have to reconsider our options," Marie said, her eyes narrowing. "But I believe he'll see the value in it. This list could expose a network of spies, and you know how the French government loves a scandal."

J.D. felt a mix of hope and apprehension. The prospect of exposing corruption within the Kremlin was enticing, but the risks were monumental. "How do we get to Philippe without drawing attention?"

Marie smiled faintly, a glint of mischief in her eyes. "That's where the game of deceit comes in. I have a plan. We'll approach him under the guise of a routine meeting about unrelated matters. He won't suspect anything until it's too late."

Irina's brow furrowed. "And what if he senses something's off?"

"Then we improvise," Marie replied, her tone unwavering. "We're operating on a need-to-know basis.

The fewer people involved, the better."

J.D. took a deep breath, trying to quell the anxiety that bubbled beneath the surface. "When do we move?"

"Now," Marie said, rising from her seat. "We don't have time to waste. The longer we linger here, the greater the chance of someone identifying us."

As they stood to leave, J.D. felt the weight of the locked box in his bag, a constant reminder of the precarious path they were walking. Together, they slipped out of the café, blending into the throngs of people on the bustling Parisian streets.

The trio moved swiftly, navigating the narrow alleys and busy sidewalks, J.D. constantly scanning their surroundings for any signs of danger. As they approached a nondescript office building, Marie led them inside, her demeanor shifting to one of calm professionalism.

"Philippe's office is on the second floor," she instructed, leading the way to an elevator. "Keep it casual. We're just here for a chat."

The elevator doors closed, and J.D. felt the tension in the air thickening. Irina stood beside him, her expression a mix of determination and anxiety. "We can do this," she whispered, her eyes steady.
When the elevator dinged, they stepped out into a starkly lit hallway lined with closed doors. Marie led them to one marked "Philippe Dubois." She knocked briskly, and a moment later, the door swung open.

Philippe was a man in his early fifties, with tousled gray hair and sharp features that spoke of a keen intellect. He wore a tailored suit that seemed slightly rumpled, as if he had been deep in thought before their arrival. His eyes flickered with curiosity as he regarded them.

"Marie, this is a surprise. What brings you here?" he asked, stepping aside to let them in.

"Philippe, thank you for seeing us," Marie replied smoothly, her tone friendly yet authoritative. "I wanted to discuss some urgent matters."

As they settled into his office, J.D. felt the tension spike. He exchanged a glance with Irina, both of them aware that the stakes were high.

"Urgent matters?" Philippe repeated, leaning back in his chair, his brow arched. "You don't usually come to me unless it's serious."

Marie maintained her composure, her voice steady. "We've come across some information that could have significant implications for national security. I thought it best to discuss it with you directly."

Philippe's interest piqued, and he leaned forward, his expression shifting to one of intrigue. "Go on."

Irina shot J.D. a quick look, silently urging him to trust her instincts. He nodded slightly, knowing this was their moment. Marie gestured for J.D. to pull out the box.

With steady hands, he placed it on the desk and opened it, revealing the carefully organized documents inside. Philippe's eyes widened as he scanned the contents.

"What is this?" he asked, a mix of disbelief and curiosity evident in his voice.

"This is a list of deep-cover Russian operatives," Irina said, her tone firm. "We believe it to be authentic, and if that's the case, it could expose a significant network operating within France and beyond."

Philippe leaned closer, examining the documents with a furrowed brow. "And how did you come by this?" Marie interjected smoothly. "That's not important right now. What is important is that we have a chance to stop something potentially catastrophic. We need your expertise to verify this."

The room fell silent as Philippe studied the papers, his expression shifting from skepticism to contemplation. Finally, he looked up, his gaze serious. "If this is real, it's explosive. But you must understand the risks involved. The Kremlin won't take kindly to this information being leaked."

"We're aware," J.D. said, his voice steady. "But we can't let fear dictate our actions. Lives are at stake."

Philippe nodded slowly, his mind clearly racing. "Alright. I'll do my part to verify this, but you need to be ready for the fallout. If this is legitimate, it will attract attention from all sides."

Irina leaned forward, her voice urgent. "We need the verification as soon as possible. Can you do that?"

"I can arrange for a secure meeting with my contacts, but it will take time," Philippe replied, his tone cautious. "I need you to lay low until then. No unnecessary risks."

As they discussed logistics, J.D. felt a sense of hope mingling with apprehension. They were walking a tightrope, and one misstep could send them tumbling into danger.

Finally, Philippe concluded, "I'll need to make some calls. You should wait here until I return. I'll instruct my assistant to keep an eye out for any unusual activity."

As they settled into a tense silence, J.D. couldn't shake the feeling that they were being watched. The stakes were high, and the game of deceit they were playing was only just beginning.

Outside, the winter sun dipped lower in the sky, casting long shadows that crept into the room, a constant reminder that in the world of espionage, nothing was ever truly as it seemed.

CHAPTER 6
THE LIST

As the muffled sounds of footsteps echoed outside the storage room, J.D. felt a wave of anxiety wash over him. He had to act quickly. Memories of his brother's death in Ukraine flooded his mind, haunting him with vivid clarity. The weight of the classified list pressed heavily in his bag, and he could feel the temptation to destroy it growing stronger.

He glanced at Irina, her eyes betraying a mix of fear and determination. She was focused on the door, ready to defend against whatever threat lay beyond. Yet, in that moment, J.D. felt the pull of his past tugging at him, urging him to make a choice.

Should I destroy it? he thought, wrestling with the idea. *Or could it be a weapon, a way to gain leverage over Irina?*

J.D. had always understood the value of information in their world, but this list was different. It contained names and details that could expose a network of spies, potentially turning the tide in a dangerous game. Yet, it also represented his brother's death, a painful reminder of everything he had lost.

He opened the box slowly, the hinges creaking, revealing the neatly organized documents. The light from the overhead bulb illuminated the names on the list, each one a ghost from his past. As he traced his fingers over the paper, the weight of guilt settled heavily on his chest.

"I can't believe we're here," he murmured, half to himself. "All because of this damned list."

Irina turned to him, her expression softening. "J.D., we need to focus. If they find us—"

"Do you ever think about how we got here?" he interrupted, his voice rising. "How we're caught in this web of deceit? The list is just a part of it —a dangerous part."

"What are you saying?" she asked, her brow furrowing.
He hesitated, weighing his words. "What if I just… burn it? Destroy it all? It might be the only way to free ourselves from this nightmare."

Irina stepped closer, her voice low but intense. "You know that's not the answer. This list could expose the corruption, save lives. You can't just throw it away because it reminds you of your brother."

J.D. felt a surge of frustration. "You don't understand! I lost everything because of this world. My brother… he tried to do the right thing, and look where it got him."

Her eyes softened, and for a moment, he saw a flicker of empathy. "I do understand, J.D. I lost someone too. But we can't let their deaths be in vain. We have to use this information to fight back."

He looked at her, feeling the weight of her words. *Could he really use the list as leverage?* The thought made his stomach turn, but it also offered a glimmer of hope. If they could expose the truth, perhaps it would bring some measure of justice—not just for his brother, but for Irina's too.

"Let's just hold onto it for now," he said reluctantly, closing the box. "But if it comes to a choice between this list and our lives, I won't hesitate."

Irina nodded, her expression resolute. "Fair enough. But we need to stay focused. We can't let our emotions cloud our judgment."

Just then, the sound of voices drew closer, and
J.D. felt his heart race. They were running out of time. "We need to find a way out of here," he urged, scanning the small room for options. Irina moved to the door, pressing her ear against it. "I hear them. We have to be smart about this."

J.D. took a deep breath, steeling himself. "Let's make a plan. We need to get to Philippe before they do." As they prepared to make their move, J.D. felt a renewed sense of purpose. The past would always haunt him, but he couldn't let it dictate his future. Together, they would navigate this treacherous path, using the shadows of their pasts as fuel to fight for a better tomorrow.

With a final glance at the box, he tucked it securely under his arm. Whatever lay ahead, he was ready to confront it—no matter the cost. Together, they would face the encroaching darkness, determined to emerge into the light.

CHAPTER 7
A COLD CONFRONTATION

The tension in the air was palpable as J.D. and Irina slipped out of the storage room, moving cautiously down the dimly lit corridor. The muffled voices outside had faded, but the sense of urgency remained. They needed to reach Philippe before their pursuers found them.

As they navigated through the maze of crates and machinery, J.D. felt a mixture of adrenaline and dread coursing through him. The weight of the classified list under his arm was a constant reminder of the stakes, and he could sense that their fragile alliance was about to be tested.

They finally reached the main entrance of the warehouse, and J.D. pushed the door open just enough to peek outside. The coast seemed clear, but he knew better than to let his guard down. "We need to move quickly," he whispered, gesturing for Irina to follow him.

As they stepped into the cold air, the shadows of the warehouse loomed behind them, a reminder of the danger that lurked just out of sight. They hurried toward Philippe's car, parked a short distance away, but just as they reached the vehicle, Irina suddenly halted.

"Wait," she said, her voice low but urgent. "We need to talk."

J.D. turned to face her, confusion etched on his features. "Now? We don't have time—"

"I know we don't have time," she interrupted, her eyes flashing with intensity. "But we can't keep pretending everything's fine. You're holding onto that list like it's your lifeline, but it's not just yours to control."

His heart raced as he felt the weight of her accusation. "What are you talking about?"

"I saw the look in your eyes back there," she pressed, stepping closer. "You want to use it as leverage against me, don't you? You think you can manipulate me because of my past."

J.D. recoiled, anger flaring within him. "That's not true! I'm trying to protect you. This list is dangerous, and you don't understand what's at stake."

Irina's expression hardened. "You think you're the only one who's suffered? I lost my brother because of this game! I'm not going to let you use that against me."

"Use it against you?" he shot back, his voice rising. "I'm trying to keep both of us alive! The last thing I want is to repeat the mistakes of the past!"

Their voices echoed in the empty parking lot, the tension crackling between them like an electric charge. J.D. felt the weight of their shared pain, but the anger clouded his judgment.

"Maybe you should think about what you're really doing," Irina continued, her voice trembling but firm. "This isn't just about you anymore. We're in this together, whether you like it or not."

J.D. took a deep breath, trying to rein in his emotions. "I know that. But I can't help but feel like you have your own agenda. How can I trust you?"

Irina stepped back, hurt flashing across her face. "Trust? That's rich coming from you. You're the one who's kept secrets, who's afraid to open up!"

The accusation stung, and for a moment, J.D. faltered. He had always been guarded, a defense mechanism born from years of betrayal. But now, faced with Irina's raw honesty, he realized how much he had held back.

"Maybe I don't know how to trust," he admitted, his voice softer. "But I want to. I'm just scared."

Irina's expression softened, a flicker of understanding passing between them. "We're both scared. But we have to lean on each other if we're going to survive this."

Just then, a noise shattered their moment of vulnerability—a distant engine revving. J.D. turned toward the sound, heart racing. "We need to go, now!"

Without another word, they sprinted toward the car, adrenaline propelling them forward. J.D. fumbled with the keys, finally managing to unlock the door just as the sound of tires screeching echoed behind them.

"I'll drive," Irina said, urgency threading her voice as she hopped into the driver's seat. J.D. slid into the passenger side, his heart pounding as he glanced back. The SUV was barreling toward them, a dark harbinger of the danger closing in.

"Go! Go!" he shouted, urging her on as she slammed her foot down on the accelerator. The car lurched forward, and they sped out of the parking lot just in time to avoid the approaching vehicle.

As they raced through the streets, J.D. felt the tension coiling between them. The confrontation lingered, unresolved but charged with the possibility of something deeper. He glanced over at Irina, who was focused on the road, her brow furrowed in concentration.

"Where to?" she asked, her voice steady despite the chaos.

"Anywhere but here," he replied, his mind racing. "We need to find Philippe and regroup."

As they navigated the winding streets of Paris, J.D. couldn't shake the feeling that they were being hunted. The SUV had vanished from view, but he knew it was only a matter of time before they were found again. "I'm sorry for what I said back there," he finally murmured, breaking the silence. "I didn't mean to—"

"No," Irina interrupted, her voice firm. "You were right to call me out. We can't afford to hide from each other. We need to be honest if we're going to make this work."

J.D. nodded, feeling a sense of relief wash over him. "Agreed. I'll do my best to be open. Just… don't let the past cloud your judgment either."

As they drove through the city, the tension began to ease, replaced by a fragile sense of camaraderie. They were two wounded souls navigating a treacherous landscape, and while trust was tenuous, it was a start.

"We'll figure this out," Irina said, determination creeping into her voice. "But we have to stick together. There's no room for doubt."

With each passing block, J.D. felt the weight of their shared burdens begin to lift, even if just a little. Together, they were stronger, and as the shadows of their pasts loomed behind them, they forged ahead into the uncertain future—united against the storm that threatened to engulf them both.

CHAPTER 8
REVELATIONS

The air inside the car was thick with a mix of tension and uncertainty as J.D. and Irina navigated the streets of Paris. J.D. glanced at Irina, her jaw set with determination. They had agreed to trust each other, but he felt the weight of secrets hanging between them—secrets that could change everything.

As they approached a quiet café near the Seine, J.D. suggested they stop for a moment to gather their thoughts. "We need to figure out our next move," he said, his voice steady despite the anxiety coursing through him.

Irina nodded, her expression thoughtful. "Let's take a moment to regroup. But we need to be quick. We can't linger."

They parked and hurried inside, the warm atmosphere offering a brief respite from the cold reality outside. They found a secluded table in the corner, the gentle hum of conversation surrounding them like a protective barrier.

"I can't shake the feeling that we're being watched," Irina said quietly, glancing around the café. "We need to stay low."

J.D. leaned in, lowering his voice. "I know. But first, we need to talk about the list. It's time we lay everything on the table."

Irina's eyes narrowed. "What do you mean?"

"I mean the truth," he replied, feeling the weight of the moment. "About your brother and everything that happened in Ukraine."

Her expression shifted, a flicker of vulnerability crossing her face. "What do you know about it?"

"Enough," he said, choosing his words carefully. "I know he was involved in something dangerous, and that it cost him his life. But there's more, isn't there?"

Irina looked down, her hands trembling slightly on the table. "I thought I could keep it buried. That if I didn't think about it, it wouldn't hurt so much."

J.D. leaned closer, sensing the crack in her armor. "You don't have to hide from me. We're in this together. If we're going to fight back, we need to understand the whole picture."

She took a deep breath, her voice barely above a whisper. "My brother was investigating a trafficking ring linked to Russian operatives. He believed he was close to uncovering something big—something that connected back to the Kremlin."

J.D. felt a chill run down his spine. "And you think the list is related?"

"Yes," Irina replied, her eyes filled with a mix of fear and determination. "I think it might contain names of people involved in that ring. But I didn't realize it until recently. I thought it was just a list of spies."

"Do you think it could lead us to his killers?" J.D. asked, his heart racing at the implications.

Irina nodded slowly. "It's possible. But uncovering that truth could put us in even more danger."

J.D.'s mind raced as he processed her words. "If we expose the trafficking ring, not only could we get justice for your brother, but we could also disrupt the Kremlin's operations."

"Exactly," she said, a glimmer of hope igniting in her eyes. "But we need to be careful. The people we are up against are ruthless."

Just then, the café door swung open, interrupting their conversation. J.D. instinctively tensed, scanning the room for any sign of danger. A group of men entered, their presence commanding and intimidating. They were dressed in dark coats, their eyes scanning the café as if searching for someone.

"Stay calm," Irina whispered, her voice steady. "We need to act natural."

J.D. nodded, forcing himself to focus. He could feel the adrenaline coursing through his veins as he watched the men approach the counter, their conversation low and conspiratorial.

"Do you think they're looking for us?" he asked, his heart pounding.

"Possibly," Irina replied, her gaze locked on the group. "We need to finish this conversation and get out of here."

"Right," J.D. said, trying to keep his voice steady. "So, what's our next move?"

Irina took a deep breath, her expression resolute. "We need to get the list to Philippe. He can help us verify the names and connect the dots. But we have to be careful. If they're onto us, we could be walking into a trap."

J.D. nodded, feeling the urgency of their situation. "Let's finish our coffee and head out the back. We can take a different route to Philippe's."

Just as they prepared to leave, one of the men from the group turned, locking eyes with J.D. A flicker of recognition crossed the man's face, and J.D. felt his stomach drop.

"Go!" he shouted, grabbing Irina's arm and propelling her toward the back exit. They slipped through the doorway just as the man called out to his companions, their voices rising in alarm.

"Stop them!" one of the men yelled, and J.D. felt panic surge through him as they burst into the alley.

"Run!" Irina urged, her voice urgent as they sprinted down the narrow passage. They could hear footsteps pounding behind them, echoing off the walls.

J.D. glanced back, catching a glimpse of the men gaining on them. "We need to split up!" he shouted. "It'll make it harder for them to follow us!"
"No!" Irina protested, fear flashing in her eyes. "We need to stick together!"

"Just trust me!" J.D. insisted. "I'll meet you at Philippe's! Go!"

With a reluctant nod, Irina veered left into another alley while J.D. continued straight ahead, his heart racing. He could hear the men closing in behind him, their shouts growing louder.

As he sprinted through the maze of streets, he pushed himself harder, adrenaline fuelling his escape. He could hear the sounds of the city around him, but all that mattered was getting to safety.

Finally, he spotted a narrow opening that led to a hidden courtyard. He darted inside, pressing himself against the wall and holding his breath as he listened for the sounds of pursuit.

The footsteps faded, and he risked a glance around the corner. The men had passed, moving in the direction Irina had taken.

Heart pounding, J.D. took a moment to collect himself. He needed to find Philippe, but first, he had to make sure Irina was safe. He quickly pulled out his phone, sending her a brief message: *I'm okay. Meet at Philippe's.*

With a surge of determination, he set off toward Philippe's location, the gravity of their situation weighing heavily on him. The list held the potential for justice, but it also put them both in grave danger.

As he navigated the streets, he couldn't shake the feeling that they were being watched. The shadows of their pasts loomed large, and the stakes had never been higher. But J.D. was ready to face whatever came next—together with Irina, they would uncover the truth and fight back against the darkness that threatened to consume them.

CHAPTER 9
ALLIES OR ENEMIES?

The sun dipped low in the sky as J.D. approached Philippe's office, the shadows lengthening around him. He could feel the weight of the day's events pressing down on him—his heart raced with the urgency of their mission. Irina was somewhere nearby, he hoped, safe from the men who had pursued them.

He pushed open the door to Philippe's office, taking a moment to catch his breath. The room was dimly lit, cluttered with papers, maps, and a large cork board covered in photographs and notes. Philippe looked up from behind his desk, concern etched on his face.

"J.D., you made it!" Philippe exclaimed, rising to greet him. "Where's Irina? I've been worried."
"She's on her way," J.D. replied, trying to mask the anxiety in his voice. "We were followed, but I think we lost them. We need to act quickly."
Philippe nodded, his expression serious. "I have a secure room in the back. We can discuss everything there."

As they moved to the back room, J.D. felt a mix of relief and dread. Time was running short, and they needed to be strategic. Once inside,

Philippe closed the door and gestured for J.D. to take a seat.

"Let's go over what you found," Philippe said, leaning forward. "Tell me everything."

J.D. hesitated for a moment, the weight of the classified list heavy in his mind. "Irina and I discovered that the list contains names linked to a trafficking ring. It's connected to her brother's investigation before he was killed."

Philippe's brow furrowed. "That's serious. Do you think it could lead us to his killers?"

"I hope so," J.D. replied. "But we need to verify the information quickly. If we can expose this ring, it could destabilize the operations of those involved."

Just then, the door swung open, and Irina rushed in, her expression a mix of determination and fear. "I'm here. What's the plan?"

"Good to see you," Philippe said, relief washing over him. "We're discussing the list and its implications. J.D. believes it could lead us to your brother's killers."

Irina's eyes widened. "That's what we need. But we have to move fast. If they discover we're onto them, it could be catastrophic."

J.D. nodded, feeling the urgency in her words. "Philippe, can you reach out to your contacts? We need to verify the names and find a way to expose them."

"Absolutely," Philippe replied, already pulling out his phone. "I have a few people I can trust. But we need to be careful. If anyone catches wind of this, we could be in serious danger."

As Philippe dialed, J.D. felt a sense of friendship growing between them. They were no longer just individuals with their own agendas; they were allies fighting against a common enemy.

"While Philippe makes those calls, we need to discuss our next steps," J.D. said, turning to Irina. "We can't just wait around. We need to be proactive."

Irina nodded, her expression resolute. "I agree. We should try to gather more information about the trafficking ring and see if we can find any leads on my brother's case."

Philippe finished his call and turned back to them. "I've contacted someone who can help us verify the names on the list. They'll meet us at a safe location in a couple of hours."

"Good," J.D. said, feeling a surge of determination. "But we can't sit idly by. We need to start piecing together the puzzle before our window closes."

Irina leaned forward, her eyes sharp. "What if we split up? I can check some contacts who might have information about the trafficking ring. You and Philippe can focus on verifying the list."
J.D. hesitated, the thought of splitting up unsettling him. "Are you sure that's wise? We don't know who's watching."

"I'll be careful," she insisted. "But we can cover more ground this way. We need to be smart about this."

Philippe nodded in agreement. "She's right. We can't afford to waste time. If we work together but separately, we increase our chances of gathering crucial information."

Reluctantly, J.D. agreed. "Alright. But stay in contact. If anything feels off, regroup immediately."

Irina smiled, a flicker of gratitude in her eyes. "We will. Let's do this."

As they made their plans, J.D. felt the stakes rising higher. The trust they were building was fragile, but necessity bound them together. They were no longer just pawns in a game —they were players, determined to expose the corruption that threatened their lives.

After finalizing their plans, Irina left to meet her contacts, while J.D. and Philippe set to work verifying the names on the list. As they pored over the documents, J.D. felt a sense of urgency. Each name represented a potential lead, a possible path to uncovering the truth.

Hours passed, the tension in the room palpable as they worked tirelessly. Philippe's phone buzzed, and he answered quickly, his expression shifting as he listened intently.

"Are you sure?" Philippe asked, his voice tight with concern. "We need to know who's involved."

After a brief exchange, he hung up and turned to J.D. "Our contact has confirmed that several names on the list are connected to high-ranking officials in both the Kremlin and various international organizations. This goes deeper than we thought."

J.D. felt a chill run down his spine. "That means we're dealing with powerful enemies. We have to be careful."

Philippe nodded, his expression grave. "If they find out we're onto them, they'll do whatever it takes to silence us."

Just then, a loud crash echoed from outside the office, followed by shouts. J.D.'s heart raced as he exchanged worried glances with Philippe. "What was that?"

"Sounds like trouble," Philippe said, moving toward the window. He peeked outside, his face paling. "They're here. We need to get out— now!"

Panic surged through J.D. as he scrambled to gather the documents. "Where's Irina?"

"I don't know," Philippe replied, urgency lacing his voice. "We have to leave before they come in."
Just as they prepared to exit, the door burst open, and a group of armed men stormed in, their faces cold and menacing. J.D. felt his heart drop.

"Hands where we can see them!" one of the men yelled, levelling a gun at them.

J.D. froze, adrenaline coursing through him. They were cornered, and the stakes had never been higher. In that instant, he realized they were not just fighting for their lives—they were fighting for the truth, for justice, and for a chance to uncover the darkness that threatened to consume them all.

As the men advanced, J.D. felt a surge of determination. They would not go down without a fight. They were allies now, bound together by a shared purpose, and he would do everything in his power to protect Irina and uncover the truth—no matter the cost.

CHAPTER 10
CHASING SHADOWS

The air was thick with tension as J.D. and Philippe stood at the back of the office, their hearts racing. The armed men advanced, closing in, and J.D. could feel the weight of the moment pressing down on him. He glanced at Philippe, who was scanning the room for an escape route.

"Follow my lead," Philippe whispered, his voice steady despite the chaos. "We'll create a distraction."

J.D. nodded, adrenaline surging. He knew they had to act fast. Just then, the loud crash of a window shattered the stillness, and shards of glass rained down. The sound drew the attention of the intruders for a split second.

"Now!" Philippe shouted.

They lunged toward the opposite side of the room, ducking behind a desk as the armed men turned their guns toward the noise. J.D.'s heart raced as he spotted an emergency exit at the far end of the room.

"Go!" he urged Philippe, pushing forward.

They sprinted toward the exit, adrenaline fuelling their escape as bullets ricocheted off the walls behind them. J.D. felt the heat of danger on his back, but they couldn't stop now—not when freedom was within reach.

They burst through the emergency exit, the cold winter air hitting them like a wall. The alleyway outside was dark and narrow, but they didn't hesitate. They ran, hearts pounding, desperate to put distance between themselves and their pursuers.

"Where's Irina?" Philippe panted, glancing back as they rounded a corner.

"I don't know!" J.D. shouted, anxiety clawing at him. "We have to find her!"

They navigated the winding streets, the sounds of pursuit fading behind them. J.D.'s mind raced with thoughts of Irina, the determination to reunite with her driving him forward.

"Let's head toward the docks," Philippe suggested, his breath coming in quick gasps. "It's less likely they'll look for us there."

"Right," J.D. agreed, pushing himself harder. "We'll find her."

As they reached the docks, the moonlight reflected off the water, casting an eerie glow. The atmosphere was tense, the cold wind biting at their skin, but the quiet offered a brief reprieve from the chaos.

J.D. scanned the area, searching for any sign of Irina. "We need to call her," he said, pulling out his phone.

Just then, Philippe's phone buzzed. He answered quickly, his expression shifting as he listened intently. "Yes, we're at the docks. Have you seen her?"

J.D. held his breath, hope and fear battling within him. But Philippe's expression grew grim. "Okay, we'll wait for you."

"What did she say?" J.D. asked, anxiety rising.

"Just that she's safe for now, but she's being followed. She's trying to lose them," Philippe replied, his voice tight.

J.D. felt a mix of relief and dread. "We can't stay here. We have to move—find a better hiding spot."

Philippe nodded, scanning the area. "There's an old warehouse nearby. We can regroup there."

They made their way to the warehouse, the sound of their footsteps echoing in the silence. Inside, the air was stale, filled with the scent of salt and rust. They moved deeper into the shadows, finding a corner to huddle in.

"Let's wait for Irina," J.D. said, trying to keep his voice steady. "We can't leave without her."

Minutes felt like hours as they waited, every sound amplifying their anxiety. J.D. replayed the events of the day in his mind, the chaos, the confrontations, and the weight of the list. They had come so far, but the fight was far from over.

Just then, the sound of footsteps approached. J.D. tensed, heart pounding. "Is that her?" he whispered.

The door creaked open, and Irina slipped inside, her expression a mixture of relief and urgency. "You made it!" she exclaimed, rushing toward them.

"Are you okay?" J.D. asked, his heart swelling with relief.

"I am, but we need to move. They're close behind me," she replied, glancing over her shoulder. "We have to find a way out of here."

Philippe stepped forward, urgency in his voice. "We need to stick together. We can't split up again."

Irina nodded, determination etched on her face. "I have a plan. There's a boat docked at the end of the pier. We can use it to get across the river."

"Let's go, then!" J.D. urged, feeling a surge of adrenaline. They followed

Irina out of the warehouse and down the pier, the cold wind biting at their faces.

As they approached the boat, J.D. could hear the distant sound of voices growing closer. "Hurry!" he urged, scrambling aboard.

Irina and Philippe followed, and they quickly untied the boat from the dock. J.D. took the helm, his hands steady on the controls as he started the engine. The sound roared to life, cutting through the tension.
"Go, go!" Irina urged, glancing back at the approaching figures.

J.D. pushed the throttle down, the boat surging forward as they sped away from the dock. The cold water splashed against them, the city lights fading into the distance.

As they made their way across the river, J.D. felt a sense of hope rising within him. They were escaping the immediate danger, but the fight was far from over. They had to expose the truth behind the list and confront the corruption that had ensnared them.

"Once we're across, we need to lay low and figure out our next move," Philippe said, his voice rising above the roar of the engine. "We can't let our guard down."

J.D. nodded, focused on the path ahead. "We'll regroup and come up with a plan. We can't let them win."

As they reached the opposite shore, J.D. slowed the boat, carefully steering it into a small inlet. They quickly secured it, heartbeats pounding in their chests as they stepped onto solid ground.

"Now what?" Irina asked, scanning the area for any signs of danger.

"First, we find somewhere to hide," J.D. suggested, looking around. "Then we can figure out how to expose the trafficking ring and those behind it."

As they moved into the shadows of the trees lining the shore, J.D. felt a renewed sense of purpose. They had faced unimaginable challenges, but they were still standing together.

"We'll get through this," he said, his voice steady. "We'll uncover the truth. Together."

Irina smiled, the flicker of hope returning to her eyes. "Together."

As they pressed forward into the darkness, the weight of their pasts still lingered, but hope glimmered on the horizon. They were allies now, bound by a shared purpose, determined to fight for justice and uncover the truth.

With each step they took, they knew the battle was far from over, but they were ready to face whatever lay ahead. The shadows of the past might haunt them, but together, they would forge a new path—a path toward redemption and justice in a world filled with shadows.

CHAPTER 11
THE RECKONING

The dawn light filtered through the dusty windows of the abandoned warehouse, casting a soft glow on the makeshift table where J.D., Irina, and Philippe gathered. The faint sound of dripping water echoed in the corners, punctuating the heavy silence that enveloped them. Tension hung in the air like a thick fog, a reminder of the stakes they faced. Clara's article had sent shockwaves through the city, igniting public outrage, but they knew the real battle was just beginning.

Philippe spread the documents across the table, his brow furrowed in concentration. "We need to act quickly," he said, his voice steady despite the gravity of their situation. "The Kremlin won't sit idle while we expose them."

Irina leaned closer, her determination shining through her eyes. "We need to get the evidence to someone who can protect it—a government official or a trustworthy journalist. Someone who can ensure it won't just disappear."

J.D. took a deep breath, feeling the weight of the moment settle heavily on his shoulders. Memories of the chaos they had endured rushed through him, but he pushed them aside to focus on the task at hand. "I know someone in the French intelligence community," he said, his voice low but resolute. "If we can reach him, he can ensure our safety and help us leak the information effectively."

Philippe nodded, a glimmer of hope flickering in his eyes. "Let's move," he urged. They quickly devised a plan to meet J.D.'s contact, knowing they had little time to spare. The urgency of their mission propelled them forward as they slipped through the streets of Paris, the morning sun rising higher in the sky.

As they approached a discreet café tucked away in a narrow alley, J.D. felt a familiar tension building in his chest. The café, with its faded awning and cracked windows, looked like a relic of a bygone era, but it served as a perfect cover for their clandestine meeting. J.D. spotted his contact, a middle-aged man named Luc, sitting at a corner table, his fingers tapping nervously against his coffee cup.

"Luc," J.D. greeted, urgency lacing his voice as he slid into the seat across from him. "We have critical information regarding the trafficking ring. It's linked to high-ranking officials."

Luc's expression shifted, his brows knitting together in concern. "I've heard whispers. The Kremlin is on high alert. What do you have?"

J.D. laid out the details, his heart racing as he recounted the evidence they had gathered—the names, the connections, and the implications of exposing an operation that spanned continents. As he spoke, he could see Luc's expression darken, the weight of their findings settling over him like a heavy cloak.

"This changes everything," Luc said finally, his voice grave. "If this information gets out, it could shake the very foundations of the Kremlin. But you need to be careful. They'll come after you."

Irina leaned in, urgency evident in her posture. "We need your help, Luc. Can you ensure this information reaches the right people? We can't let it fall into the wrong hands."

Luc took a moment, his gaze shifting as he considered their request. "I'll do what I can, but you need to go into hiding until it's safe. I can arrange for a safe house, but you must stay off the radar."

As they left the café, J.D. felt a surge of hope mixed with anxiety. They had taken a significant step toward justice, but the danger was far from over. The streets felt alive around them, but J.D. couldn't shake the feeling that they were being watched. He glanced over his shoulder, scanning the crowd for any sign of trouble.

"Stay close," he murmured to Irina and Philippe, who nodded in agreement. Together, they navigated the winding streets, a whirlwind of uncertainty swirling around them.

The plan was set, but as they moved through the city, J.D. couldn't shake the feeling that this was only the calm before the storm. The shadows of their pasts loomed large, and the fight for justice had only just begun.

CHAPTER 12
A NEW DAWN

Days transformed into weeks, each moment stretching like the shadows that accompanied J.D., Irina, and Philippe. They lay low in a modest apartment in a quiet district of Paris, far from the vibrant noises of the city. The walls, once adorned with cheerful paintings, now felt like a cage, echoing their anxieties and fears. The tension in the air was palpable, thick enough to cut through, yet they remained united, bound by a shared purpose.

Each morning, J.D. would wake before dawn, the first light filtering through the grimy windows, casting a dim glow across the room. He would sit by the window, the chill of the early morning air brushing against his skin, contemplating the weight of the world they carried. Outside, the city stirred to life, oblivious to the storm brewing just beneath the surface.

Finally, after what felt like an eternity, Luc reached out with news that stirred a flicker of hope in their weary hearts. "The evidence has been secured, and the investigation is underway. The Kremlin's influence is being challenged."

Relief washed over them like a tide, but J.D. knew better than to let his guard down. "What about us?" he inquired, his voice steady despite the racing of his heart.

"You're safe for now," Luc assured, his tone serious. "But you should consider leaving Paris. The situation is still volatile."

The mention of escape sparked a fire of defiance in Irina. "We can't run forever. We need to continue the fight for justice," she asserted, her eyes blazing with conviction.

J.D. felt a swell of admiration for her tenacity. "You're right. But we can't do it here—not yet," he replied, scanning the cramped apartment for a way forward.

As they gathered around the table, the atmosphere shifted. They made plans to relocate to a more secure base, a place where they could continue gathering intel and collaborate with allies. The tension of their shared pasts hung heavy, but now they stood on the precipice of a new beginning.

Days later, they set out at dawn, the streets still cloaked in a soft fog that blurred the edges of reality. They navigated through back alleys and side streets, each corner revealing the city's hidden secrets. J.D. felt a renewed sense of purpose, the weight of their mission pressing firmly against his chest. The shadows of their pasts had haunted them long enough; it was time to confront the darkness head-on.

As they arrived at their new location —a safe house nestled in the outskirts of the city—J.D. was struck by a sense of foreboding. The house, though unassuming, held a history of its own, its walls whispering tales of those who had come before. It was here they would continue their fight.

Inside, J.D. surveyed their surroundings, the air thick with anticipation. "This place has potential," he said, his mind racing with possibilities. "We can set up a command center, coordinate with our contacts, and stay one step ahead of our enemies."

Irina nodded, her expression resolute. "And we'll need to establish a network of allies. If the investigation gains traction, we'll need people on the ground who can provide intel."

Philippe chimed in, his voice steady. "I can reach out to some trusted contacts in the intelligence community. They might be able to assist us in monitoring the Kremlin's reaction to the investigation."

As they plotted their next steps, J.D. felt a sense of camaraderie growing between them. They had fought against the shadows of their pasts, and together, they would continue to shine a light on the truth, determined to make a difference in a world filled with uncertainty.

But lurking beneath their resolve was the knowledge that danger was never far behind. J.D. couldn't shake the feeling that their enemies were watching, waiting for the perfect moment to strike. The stakes were higher than ever, and the shadows were closing in.

With hope in their hearts and a fierce resolve, they stepped into the dawn of a new era, ready to confront whatever lay ahead. They understood that the fight for justice was just beginning, and the true reckoning was yet to come. As they prepared to face the challenges ahead, J.D. felt a spark of determination ignite within him. This was their moment to turn the tide, to reclaim their lives from the clutches of darkness.

And as the sun broke through the fog, casting golden rays across the landscape, J.D. knew they would not back down. They were warriors in a battle for the truth, and they would shine a light on the shadows that threatened to consume them.

© 2024 Jerry B. Marchant
Publisher : BoD · Books on Demand,
31 avenue Saint-Rémy, 57600 Forbach,
bod@bod.fr
Print : Libri Plureos GmbH,
Friedensallee 273, 22763 Hamburg
(Allemagne)
ISBN : 978-2-3225-7007-2
Dépôt légal : Mars 2025